REVENGE OF THE
DINNER LADIES

**Also by the same author,
and available in Knight Books:**

THE HEADMASTER WENT SPLAT!
THE CASE OF THE FEEBLE WEEBLE
THE SCOURGE OF THE DINNER LADIES
THE DINNER LADIES CLEAN UP

Revenge of the Dinner Ladies

David Tinkler

Illustrated by David McKee

KNIGHT BOOKS
Hodder and Stoughton

A catalogue record for this book is
available from the British Library

ISBN 0-340-56809-7

Printed and bound in Great Britain for
Hodder and Stoughton Paperbacks, a
division of Hodder and Stoughton Ltd.,
Mill Road, Dunton Green, Sevenoaks,
Kent TN13 2YA. (Editorial Office: 47
Bedford Square, London WC1B 3DP)
by Clays Ltd, St Ives plc.

Chapter 1

This wild child is the proud owner of the world's weirdest laugh; it sounds exactly like water whirling and swirling out of a bath, which is why they call him Plughole.

I am sure that you are a most brilliant and talented young person. Am I right?

Good.

Well, a deeply brilliant, highly talented young person like yourself could laugh a whirling, swirling, Plughole-style laugh, couldn't you? Go on. Try it.

Now that is almost exactly how Plughole

laughed at a dinner lady at his school – only louder and longer and wilder and stronger. He'd been sitting, you see, having his dinner at Littlebampton County Primary School, when Granny Fang, the school cook, had come into the hall to croak insults at the other dinner ladies.

'Slow,' she'd croaked at Mrs Slow, the dimmest dinner lady, 'you've got a face like an empty loo – completely vacant!'

That is when Plughole had laughed; whirls and swirls of hoots and honks had sprung out of his huge mouth. Granny Fang glared at him. 'What should we do with a boy that cheeks us?' she growled.

'Boil him,' cackled Batty, the merriest dinner lady.

'Skin him,' roared Sludge, the one that never smiled but frowned forever fiercely.

'Then,' said Slow, the thick one, slowly, 'when the boy is boiled and skinned we could fry him. Boy-burgers might be nice,' said Slow happily, 'with jam. Or we could just eat his feet – shredded feet's my favourite.'

Plughole waited and worried. The new dinner ladies were always talking about cooking children with apples in their mouths and serving them up with onion sauce, but they were not really allowed to do it. He glanced at Granny Fang with her shark-teeth and merciless eyes, at Mrs Sludge with her hard, angry, boot face, at Mrs Slow with her empty loo expression, and at little Batty. Plughole could tell by the way she was grinning that Batty actually quite liked children – particularly if they were perky like himself. Yet her wild ways worried him.

'Batty,' croaked the cook, 'nip into the kitchen and get a pan of soup. Bring it 'ere and empty it over this boy – he has to be taught manners!'

Chapter 2

Plughole laughed all the way home on the school bus. All around him chortling children sniggered and grinned. 'Well done, Plughole!' one of them managed to gasp.

'Brilliant!' sighed another.

'I didn't do anything,' honked young Plug whirlingly, 'I just sat there waiting for her to empty the soup over my head...'

'Then old Phartalot came in,' gurgled a girl.

'Yes,' agreed another, 'he came pacing in all importantly and he looked at Batty with the pan in her hand and he looked at Plughole sort of cowering there waiting to be spurtled and he went sort of stern and grim...'

'Who did?' asked a senior infant.

'Old Phartalot – the Headteacher – he went all important and spoke in his headteachering voice to Batty: I HOPE YOU DO NOT INTEND TO WASTE A WHOLE PAN OF NOURISHING SOUP BY THROWING IT OVER A BOY, MISS BATTY – that's what he said...'

'And what did Batty say?'

'She said, NO...' the girl began to reply.

'She said, I SHOULD THINK NOT,'

corrected another girl, 'I WOULD NOT DREAM OF SUCH A THING, she said, NOT WHEN I COULD EMPTY IT OVER A WEIRDO AND A WALLY!'

'Then old Phartalot blinked,' continued a third year boy.

'Yes. He blinked a baffled blink in a puzzled way and he said, WHAT WEIRDO?'

'And Batty sprang onto a table...'

'And she shrieked...'

'YOU ARE THE WEIRDO, PHARTALOT, AND YOU'RE THE WALLY TOO...'

'Then she emptied the soup all over his head...'

The bus rocked with laughter, even the driver was in hysterics, and loud, long, and madly strong, Plughole's bath-laugh boomed above the rest.

What a way to end the term!

'I'll miss the dinner ladies,' grinned a girl.

'Yes, it's a pity they've all been sacked,' mused her friend, 'they sort of livened things up.'

'Well, we'll never see them again,' laughed Plughole who had reached his stop and was walking towards the door. ''Bye everyone, see you in September!'

The laughing lad clambered down from the bus and waved until it turned a corner. Then

he opened an impressive pair of rusty ga~
and began to plod down a long drive towards
a huge house. In fact there were *two* drives
running along beside each other; one was the
main drive which led to the front door and
was for posh people to use; the other ended
up round the back – and was for riff-raff.

Plughole tramped along the posh drive
swinging his bulging end-of-term school bags
and kicking stones, but when he got near to
the house itself – where its stern windows could
see him – he nipped over a hedge onto the
other drive so as to go round the side and in
at the back. Plughole was riff-raff and was not
allowed to come in by the front like his
cousins.

Blight Hall's huge kitchens were eerily
empty. There was no cook or kitchen maid,
only a cat asleep by the iron stove. Plughole
had filled that stove with coal before setting
off for school and now he had to top it
up – but not until after he'd boiled the kettle
for tea.

The boy worked briskly, filling the black
kettle from a brass tap, making the tea in a
silver teapot, filling the scuttle with coal,
topping up the stove. It was as if he was
frightened of being told off if he was slow.

Then a bell rang.

There was a series of bells on the kitchen wall, all marked with the names of the rooms of the posh parts of the house, but Plughole didn't have to look at the wall to know who was ringing. He quickly loaded a tray with tea things and added a plate of sandwiches; he'd not had to make them that day because he'd swapped three marbles for some at school; they'd got a bit fluffy in his pocket but, after a gentle scrubbing with a washing-up brush, they looked quite fresh.

'Plughole!' screamed a voice from upstairs. The little lad stuck his tongue out of his wide mouth and made a face. Then, carefully carrying the loaded tray, he left the kitchens, crossed the great hall, and began to climb the stairs.

'Plughole!' screamed the voice. 'If you don't bring me my tea this minute, I'll pack you straight back to that orphanage!'

Chapter 3

It's always difficult opening doors when you're holding a tray. Plughole had to put it down, swing the bedroom door open, and then pick it up again.

'What *are* you doing?' called his aunt. She was sitting up in bed surrounded by pads of paper, boxes of chocolates, and books.

Plughole didn't reply but concentrated on not spilling as he placed the tray on the bedside table while his aunt scrutinised the sandwiches.

'Well,' she said, 'your bread cutting has improved since yesterday. What's inside them?' Fortunately she didn't stop for an answer because Plughole had forgotten to ask and didn't know. She darted out a plump hand full of rings and jangling with bracelets, clutched a sandwich, hoisted it towards her chubby chops and chewed.

'This is revolting!' she spluttered. 'Cornflakes and HP sauce! Is that your idea of a joke?'

'No Aunt Amelia, I – I thought you'd like them.'

'Well I don't. Really, Plughole, after all I've done for you I have a right to expect a little consideration.'

'Yes, Aunt Amelia.'

'It's not as if I ask much of you, simply to do the grass and the flowerbeds and keep the house clean and rustle up the odd meal until we get a new set of servants.'

'Yes, Aunt Amelia. I'm sorry about the sandwiches.'

'You remind me very much of a character in one of my books,' replied the aunt, popping a choc into her chops to take away the taste of the sauce and cornflake sandwich. 'It was one of my first books, I'm sure you've read it — *Jolly Japes at St. Ursula's* — the first St. Ursula book. Well, the St. Ursula girls meet this ragged waif. Plughole, do you know what a waif is?'

'No, Aunt.'

'You, Plughole, are a waif. A waif is a sort of orphan. Understand?'

'But, I'm...'

'— Well, this ragged waif was called Willy, Willy the Waif, and he lived in an old Mini. The girls tried to befriend him and teach him table manners and macramé but he was too clumsy to cotton on. He tried his best in a heartwarming way, but things always turned out wrong for him. And that's like you, isn't it? Trying to be helpful. Making sandwiches

14

for me so that I don't have to stop work – but filling them with muck!'

'Sorry...'

'You mean well, Plughole. But you are stupid.'

'I...'

'You can't help it. It's heredity – your father was stupid and your mother was stupid to run off with him.'

'But...'

' – Do you know what your father did for a living?'

'Yes, of course...'

'Don't interrupt. He was a clown, Plughole, in a circus. Imagine that! My sister running off with a circus clown! The disgrace! And then they both went and – well – we won't talk about it except to say it was an extraordinarily *stupid* thing to do – as well as very wicked. And, of course, everyone talked about that too. The *shame*, Plughole, that your unfortunate mother brought to this family.'

'I'm sorry, Aunt.'

'And when you were put in that orphanage people went about saying I was *heartless* – me, Plughole, *heartless*!' She stuffed another chocolate into a cheek and continued indignantly, 'I am *not* heartless, Plughole, I took you out of the orphanage and into my home, didn't I?'

'Yes, Aunt Amelia.'

'So now no one can say that Amelia Blight is too snobbish to have anything to do with you because it just isn't true. I care for you, Plughole, very deeply. Not as deeply as I care for your dear cousins, of course, but then they are my own children, and clever, graceful, and well-mannered and beautiful with mouths that are not deformed and their father was a most respectable man who died in a most respectable way — shot by a bishop — something that can happen to anyone.' Amelia Blight was going to explain how it had been an accident and how the bishop had mistaken her husband for a huge rabbit, when the telephone beside her rang.

'Yes...yes...yes...' she said. 'I *have* got an advertisement in the *Littlebampton Gazette*. I *am* looking for staff including a cook — what? Four of you, yes, a trained team! Can you cook? What was that? *Posh nosh* did you say? Excellent. When can you start?'

'Was that someone answering the advertisement?' asked Plughole when she'd put the receiver down.

'Yes it was,' replied his aunt with satisfaction. 'We've a whole new team of servants who'll start tomorrow, cook, chauffeur, the lot. Just in time!'

'Just in time for what?'

'In time for your cousins coming home from school; they'll be here tomorrow evening and you, Plughole, can go down to the station with the new chauffeur to meet them. You can help with the luggage.'

Chapter 4

Laugh the Plughole laugh again.

Brilliant! It is a very loud laugh, isn't it? No wonder everyone on the station turned round to stare and glare. Plughole had been standing there, you see, under the station clock quietly grinning a melon-slice grin as a train rattled into the station. Two girls could be seen looking out of one of its windows. 'It's Plughole!' squawked one of them as the train stopped. A door flew open, the two girls tumbled gracefully to the platform in a heap of bags and cases, and the one that leapt up first yelled, 'Give us one of your laughs!'

So he did.

The sniffy serious people who had glared and stared when they heard the lad's loud laugh stayed glaring and staring while the two well-mannered girls pranced round the boy wo-wo-woing like a pair of Red Indians. Then they kissed him.

It was thirteen long weeks since these serious and dignified young ladies had heard Plughole's famous laugh; they'd been locked up, you see, at Trevelyan College, the poshest girls' school in all England. Being in a posh

girls' school is a bit like being in prison —
except that the food is worse; no wonder they
were prancing about full of fizz.

'Where's Mum?' asked Delia when they had
finished their war dance.

'She's not been kidnapped, has she?' cried
Jane hopefully.

'She's not mysteriously disappeared without leaving any clue?' asked Delia.

'No,' replied the grinning lad shaking his head.

'Well, where is she?'

'Working.'

'Of course,' groaned Delia.

'She sent me to meet you with one of the new servants,' explained Plughole with a cheerful smirk.

'New servants?'

'Yeh,' laughed the Plughole swirlingly and whirlingly. 'Wait till you meet them – you'll wish you'd stayed at school!'

Chapter 5

A huge hag with tiger eyes and a snout was waiting for them by the Rolls Royce.

'This is Sludge,' grinned Plughole. 'She's the new chauffeur.'

'Hello, Sludge, pleased to meet you,' giggled the girls politely.

'Good evening, young ladies. If you'd like to get into the back, I'll tuck you up with a travelling rug.'

'Don't bother about that, Sludge, just bung the bags into the boot and head for home. I'm famished!'

'So am I,' agreed Jane. 'Do we have a new cook?'

'Yes, Miss. She's at home cooking your dinner.'

'But what happened to the old servants?' asked Delia.

'They asked for more money,' explained Plughole, 'so your mum sacked them. Then she got into the most awful strop because there was no one to wait on her or make her meals or fuss over her. She had me mopping and dusting and boiling eggs and stuff until today, when Sludge and Co. arrived.'

'Where did you come from, Sludge?' asked Delia when the new chauffeur had climbed into the driver's seat.

'From Littlebampton Primary School, Miss, we was all dinner ladies there till we had a disagreement – about soup – with Mr Phartalot. Then we seen your mother's advert, Miss, for domestic staff, and Granny says, "That's the place for us," she said, "a posh house where the kids ain't cheeky."'

'Well,' warbled Delia gravely, 'The Hall is certainly posh, but I fear you may be disappointed by Plughole. He can be terribly cheeky. Still I expect your hard years as dinner ladies will have trained you in dealing with boys like him.'

'Yeh,' agreed Sludge, 'don't worry about that, Miss, we can handle Master Plughole all right. We've met him before.'

The other new servants were lined up by the front door ready to meet the girls when they arrived at Blight Hall. It was an eerie experience because the first dinner lady, nearest the door, looked just like Old Mother Hubbard – until she smiled showing sharp, filed teeth.

'Welcome 'ome,' she croaked. 'I'm your mum's new cook; Granny they call me – Granny Fang. And this here is Slow. Slow by

23

name and slow by nature, ain't yer, Slow?'

'What?' blinked the large, pudding-faced maid who stood next to her.

'Say hullo to the young ladies, Slow,' croaked Granny.

'Hull-o, young ladies,' said the maid – slowly.

'And this little one is Batty. She is the one that will be looking after you girls. I'm the cook; Sludge is the driver; Slow is the maid-of-all-work; and Batty is the lady's maid what'll comb yer 'air.'

'We'll comb our own hair,' squeaked Jane quickly, 'we wouldn't want to put Batty to any extra trouble – she'll have her hands full looking after my mother.'

'It won't be no trouble, Miss. I got a extension to the Hoover what'll do it in a twinkling,' cried little Batty eagerly.

But the introductions were cut short by a yell from upstairs. Amelia Blight, the famous writer, was calling.

'Fang?' she screamed. 'Have those girls arrived? Is that them chattering? If so – send them to me at once!'

Chapter 6

'Now look here you two,' said Amelia Blight when the girls arrived in her bedroom. 'I'm just starting another Belinda Batt adventure – I shall finish it at exactly 2.15 next Friday when I will immediately start another *Fourth Form at St. Ursula's* book, so I will want you to tell me all the japes and wheezes girls at your school got up to last term so that I can put them into it.'

'Yes, Mum.'

'Only I hope you didn't do anything naughty yourselves.'

'No, Mum.'

'Good. Now, the boy will be camping out tonight – as the weather's turned wet. Belinda Batt goes camping, you see, on Muckdrood Moor during the winter, so I want some details – like what it's like with rain seeping in through holes in the tent. Sludge is going to do some jabbing with a garden fork.'

'What? Jab Plughole?'

'No. The tent. Run along now, I'm terribly busy.'

'Won't you be coming down for supper, Mum?'

26

'No, child, but the new servants will look after you. They are very good – much better than the old ones – *so* obliging.'

'But they used to be dinner ladies,' wailed Delia.

'So what?' asked her mother.

'Well, what will Fang's cooking be like? Will we have to eat *school dinners* all the time?'

'Don't be silly.'

The dignified young ladies galloped gracefully out of their mother's bedroom and quietly slammed the door.

I am very much afraid that the teachers at Trevelyan College did not share Amelia Blight's high opinion of *The Blighters* – as the Blight twins were called. They called Jane 'the Terror' and Delia 'the Menace' because of the keen and industrious way they both worked at japes and wheezes. These girls were experts at apple-pie beds, midnight feasts, mouse-larking (which is leaving a mouse in a teacher's handbag) and all manner of japes. It was their ambition when they grew up to run a joke factory; this is why they were so learned in the use of farting powder, itching cream, and whacky soap.

'Gosh! My guts!' squawked Jane when the Blighters were safely out of their mother's earshot. 'They're rumbling and grumbling like an earthquake! I hope Fang can cook properly.'

'So do I,' prattled her sister merrily.

Downstairs, in the kitchens, the new cook was skilfully poking hot bangers into a mound of mashed potato. 'Slow!' she barked.

'Yeh.'

'Bong the gong!' Slow waddled obediently into the hall to bang the gong for dinner.

'Not with your head,' cackled little Batty, who was crossing the hall.

'You hit it with that little stick...that's right!'

Mrs Fang, with her cook's mob-cap over her head, carried the steaming mound of bangers and mash into the dining room.

'Sludge,' she croaked, 'make sure Master Plughole has washed 'is 'ands, and, if 'e 'asn't, scrub 'em with a brillo pad.'

Fortunately Plughole's hands were spotless because he'd been cleaning out the goldfish. When the inspection was complete, the three children sat down at one end of the long table.

'These bangers are frightfully good,' drawled Delia. 'Nicely charred like bangers ought to be.'

'And the mashed potato is a really beautiful colour – rosy red,' smiled Jane. 'Granny Fang must have mixed tomato ketchup in with it. What a brilliantly creative idea!'

Slow blinked a puzzled blink. Granny hadn't mixed ketchup with the mash; she'd had a nose-bleed. Slowly, the maid-of-all-work opened her mouth to correct the young lady but slowly closed it again; servants weren't supposed to talk unless they were spoken to – that's what Granny and Batty kept telling her. So she kept quiet.

The bangers and mash were followed by a luscious chocolate pudding.

'What's this?' asked Plughole. 'It tastes really scrummy!'

'It – is – choc – lot – sur – prise,' said Slow with her dur-voice; she was the only servant left waiting at table.

'Well tell Fang that it was a very pleasant surprise,' laughed Jane.

'Yes,' agreed Delia, 'please congratulate her.'

Slow waddled away down the corridors that led to the kitchens. Granny Fang was sitting comfortably in a rocking chair puffing a fag. 'The children sent me to...to congrattle you. They liked the choc-lot surprise. They was surprised how scrummy it was.'

'They'd be surprised if they knew what was in it,' chuckled Granny.

You might like to try chocolate surprise yourself; here's the recipe:

Chocolate Surprise
1 lb maggots
1/2 lb mouse droppings
1 lb chocolate
4 tablespoons of rum

Purée the maggots. Melt the chocolate and mix in. Add the rum and mouse droppings. Spit into it a couple of times. Mix well. Serves four.

'Where are you going, Batty?' asked the smiling cook as the little lady's maid lugged the Hoover out of a cupboard.

'The girls are going to bed, Granny, they're tired after their journey; I'm just off to do their hair!'

Chapter 7

'It's time for her ladyship's cup of coffee,' croaked Granny Fang when Batty returned from hoovering the girls' hair and tucking them up for the night. She handed the frisky little lady's maid a steaming cup of coffee.

'Did you make it with the right sort of water?' asked Batty. 'She won't drink tap water.'

'I know she won't. She's got to have spring water.'

'And is this made from spring water?'

''Course it is! It's the same spring water I washed my feet in. I saved it specially.'

'That's all right then,' cackled Batty. She placed the coffee on a silver tray and took it upstairs for Amelia Blight. 'She's daft, her upstairs,' she chuckled when she returned to the kitchen. 'Sitting up in bed she is reading fan letters. "Do you like your coffee, madam?" I asks 'er. "Yes," she says, "it has got a wonderful, nutty flavour!"'

'She liked the taste?'

'Yes she did. I expect she'll ring for another cup.'

'I'll have to keep washin' my feet!'

'Yeh,' laughed Batty, 'or, better still, we could ask Sludge to take a bath!'

'What?' roared Sludge from her chair by the stove.

'Nothing, dear, nothing. Go back to sleep.'

'It's a laugh being servants,' grinned Granny Fang, 'cooking posh nosh; callin' them 'orrible little kids *Master* this and *Miss* that.'

'And it's a cosy little number,' Batty pointed out. 'Plenty of booze, nice snug kitchen, not much to do...'

'S'all right for you lot,' grumbled a slow voice from a dark corner. 'But I have to work all the time. Look at me now – why do I have to do all this ironing?'

''Cos you're the maid-of-all-work,' explained Batty. 'Maids-of-all-work do all the work.'

'Well,' grumbled Slow, 'it's not fair. You're the lady's maid – you should iron the ladies' clothes.'

'Lady's maids don't iron clothes,' laughed Batty scornfully. 'Not even ladies' clothes. Lady's maids are too refined and delicate to do anything but hoover lady's hair and bring 'em plates of muffins. Besides, I gotta keep my hands lookin' nice so I can't do rough work like washing and ironing.'

'You could wear gloves.'

'Don't be daft!'

33

'Cheer up, Slow,' barked Granny, 'you, Batty and me can take the rest of the evening off. Sludge can be on duty all by herself; the rest of us can get the bikes out and go for a bit of a burn up!'

Chapter 8

As is the fashion with dinner ladies, Granny, Batty and Slow wore horned helmets and hurtled along on their motor-bikes in V-formation with Granny racing ahead in the middle of the road, Slow in the left-hand lane and Batty on the outside facing the oncoming traffic.

Charging along at 120 mph down the wrong side of the road was the sort of spree little Batty needed after a day being a lady's maid. She was a most skilful actress and could always pretend to be quiet and sensible if she had to, but there was a lot of fizz inside her which got bottled up and made her extra wild when she went back to being her real self.

No one back at Blight Hall had heard the dinner ladies depart; they'd free-wheeled silently down the drive before starting their engines, but they forgot to be quiet on their way back – roaring right up the drive to the sheds where they kept their bikes hidden.

Plughole sat up. It was dark in his tent but he had a luminous Snoopy watch which said half past twelve. Outside the roar of engines suddenly stopped. Plughole listened.

Voices.

He could hear voices – snatches of talk – a laugh. Then a door slammed and there was silence.

What was going on? Plughole was the sort of boy that went about with his ears and eyes open. He was inquisitive. Curious. He liked to find out. Quietly he slipped out of the tent and padded barefoot over the wet grass to the kitchen door. There was laughter, muffled but merry, coming from the kitchens. Had thieves broken in?

He peeped through the key-hole into the back-kitchen; no one was there. Silently he turned the handle and stepped softly over the flag-stones towards the door that led to the front kitchen. That is where the chattering was coming from; light shone under the door. Plughole placed an eager eye at the key-hole – it was only the dinner ladies cackling at each other as they sat about drinking.

'Batty 'ad a spot of bother,' croaked Granny Fang's voice; Plughole couldn't see her face but she winked at Batty as she spoke and stretched out an arm to refill her glass with gin.

'She went round Sainsbury's,' said Slow's dur-voice. 'It was late night shopping.'

'What's wrong with that?' snorted Sludge.

36

'People are always going round Sainsbury's. That's what supermarkets are for – going round!'

There was a short silence after this scornful outburst. Granny gazed into the dying embers of the kitchen fire, sighed, sipped her drink and continued. 'Well,' she croaked, 'Batty went round Sainsbury's on her motor-bike.'

'What!'

'Knockin' down tins,' chuckled Batty happily.

'Helping herself to booze,' croaked Granny.

'Singing a little song,' laughed Batty.

'Shovin' a skinhead into a freezer,' sighed Granny.

'To cool him down,' smiled Batty.

'Then she snatched a handful of cash from the checkout,' continued Granny gravely. 'After that she rode out the shop and drove into the cinema.'

'She went on the stage when the film was going on,' said Slow, 'and joined in. Batman it was – Batman and Batty – only the audience didn't like it.'

'The coppers came,' growled Granny.

'They chased us,' explained Slow, 'and Granny chucked a brick at them.'

'What!' roared Sludge. 'You mean you've been chased by the police?'

'All over the place,' squawked Batty gleefully. 'We led 'em a right dance before we shook 'em off.'

'They didn't chase you back here, did they? They don't know you live here, do they?'

'No,' replied Granny. 'Give us some credit, Sludge. But we'd better be careful, they might come sniffing about these parts...'

'But we were going to stay here *quietly* for months,' hissed Sludge angrily. 'It's a cosy little number. We were going to stay here pretending to be servants and go out late at night burgling...'

'We can still go burgling,' laughed Batty.

'Not if half the police force in the county is out looking for us we can't.'

'Don't worry,' croaked Granny calmly. 'Relax. We'll still go burgling like we planned. As a matter of fact I've a good idea for the next job...'

But the other dinner ladies were not listening. They were looking at the kitchen door — which was opening!

Chapter 9

'Thieves!' cackled little Batty. 'That's a good one, Master Plug! He thinks we're thieves, girls!'

Granny and Sludge hissed, honked and shuddered with laughter, while Slow looked blank. 'But I thought we were thieves,' she said with her puzzled dur-voice. 'I thought we went round burgling...' But Slow's words were drowned by hysterical giggles; tears were rolling down Granny Fang's face – she wept with laughter.

'Oh you are a *scream*, Slow,' shrieked Batty.

''Course we go round burgling,' croaked Granny. 'But that don't mean we're thieves!'

'Yes it does,' spluttered Plughole.

He was standing in the middle of the kitchen in his ragged pyjamas and cold bare feet looking frail and pale. Being Plughole he'd just barged into the kitchen savage and mad when he'd heard the dinner ladies plotting, whereas a wise and cautious child would simply have tip-toed away and told someone about it. But young Plughole was not always wise or cautious; sometimes he was brash, rash and full of dash. Now he didn't know

what was going to happen to him and waves of worry were tumbling and rumbling his guts; his eyes were wide and his hands wet with sweat.

'Bless his little heart,' chuckled Batty. 'I suppose we'd better tell him – only you must promise to keep this a secret, Master Plug – we're police agents...'

'*Police*?'

'Yeh,' grunted Sludge.

'From Scotland Yard,' explained Batty. 'We've been sent down from London *in disguise* to check up on the local coppers...'

'They're not much cop, you see,' croaked Granny.

'They should be sacked,' agreed Sludge.

'So we've been sent to *test* them,' Batty continued earnestly.

'Test them?' gasped the bewildered boy.

'Yeh, test 'em by unleashing a crime wave,' croaked Granny Fang with her dangerous grin, 'to see how long it takes 'em to track us down. Here, if you don't believe us, look at this!' Granny brandished an important card in front of the Plug's snub nose. BUSS PASS, it said. 'Do you know what that stands for?'

'No.'

'I'd 'ave thought it was obvious – Burgling Undercover Super Squad. Police Agents –

Strictly Secret. That's who we are – the undercover super-squad from Scotland Yard! See?'

'Not servants?'

'No,' they laughed.

'Not dinner ladies?' They shook their heads.

'Sit down, Master Plughole,' croaked Granny gently. 'Now, you must tell no one about this operation – not yer aunt, not the other kids. Nobody.'

'Okay,' promised the Plughole faithfully. Then a smile spread slowly across his solemn face like sunshine spreading across a meadow. 'Hey,' he suddenly exclaimed. 'Can I help? Can I be an undercover agent too?'

Granny Fang shook her head and was about to tell the little lad, kindly but firmly, that he was too young for such dangerous and important work, when Batty darted forward and whispered eagerly into her earhole. Granny listened gravely. 'Very well, Master Plughole, so long as you promise to obey orders you can help us.'

'You mean I can go burgling!' cried the young lad keenly.

'Exactly. Only you must hand over everything you nick to me, Plughole, you mustn't keep it for yourself – that would be against the law. Understand?'

'Yes. Of course.'

'Here, in this house, you must treat us as servants just as usual. But when we are out burgling you must call Slow – Constable Slow, understand?'

'Yes.'

'And Sludge you call Sergeant, see?'

'Yes.'

'And Batty you call Inspector Batty, got that?'

'Inspector Batty.'

'That's right. And I'm Detective Chief Superintendent Fang – Fang of the Yard. You can call me *Chief*!'

'When do I start, Chief?' asked the excited boy.

'Tomorrow.'

Chapter 10

'Now, Master Plughole,' croaked the Detective Chief, 'a keen young agent like yourself should keep his eye on Inspector Batty. You'll learn a lot off of her; she's artful, Batty is. She has a natural bent.'

'For what?' cried Plughole in his sudden, eager, blurting voice.

'For crime,' replied Granny huskily. She always spoke like a frog with another frog in its throat. 'If Batty weren't honest, she could be one of the most brilliant crooks in the world. So you watch her cunning ways—specially in the snatching line.'

'Snatching?' yelped the wondering boy. 'What's that?'

Granny popped a slice of fried bread into her shark mouth and chewed it for a while before answering. It was just after breakfast, you see, the morning after they'd told Plughole about being agents; he was sitting in the big kitchen with Granny Fang while Slow was washing up in the scullery.

'There's all sorts of snatching, Master Plug, pick-pocketing, bag-grabbing, steaming, or the old pram-scam...'

'Pram-scam?' warbled the eager lad.

'Sludge is out in the workshop doing up a pram right now. She found one in the wood shed – you're going to be sitting in it soon.'

'I wouldn't fit.'

'You'll fit all right when Sludge has finished with it. She's good with prams, Sludge is. Mark you, all she's got to do is kick out the bottom – which is well within her scope. Finish that 'orrible tin of condensed milk and come and see.'

'Okay.'

The young secret agent of police followed the Chief as she lumbered out of the back door, across the yard and into the workshop next to the garages where all Amelia Blight's cars were kept. Sludge was out there gazing proudly at an old pram.

'Well, Master Plug,' croaked Granny, 'what does that look like?'

'Just a pram. An ordinary pram!'

'Look under it; what can you see?'

'A cardboard box.'

'Exactly,' nodded Granny Fang,'– an ordinary pram with a huge, big cardboard box squashed in on the pram tray underneath. If you saw a lady pushing that down the street you wouldn't look twice, would you?'

'No.'

'Now look inside the pram...that's right, take the cover off.'

Plughole unhooked one of the loops that kept the pram's cover on, peeled it back and looked inside. 'The bottom's been taken out!' he cried. 'I can see right through to the cardboard box.'

'Keep your voice down,' hissed Sludge with a glare.

'Sorry.'

'Now,' croaked Granny, 'climb inside – I'll hold it steady – that's right. See, you can sit right down in the cardboard box. Now, when I pull up the hood – like that – and put the cover back again and hook it up like it was raining – then no one would know there was a boy in there, would they?'

'No.'

'From out here,' explained Granny's husky voice, 'it looks just like a pram with a box of groceries stuffed under it. Look at the sides – that's right, by your shoulders – what do you see?'

'Flaps,' cried the Plughole in surprise. 'What are they for?'

'For snatching through of course,' growled Sludge.

'You stick your hand through a flap, Master Plug, when you want to nick something,'

explained Granny. 'Clever isn't it? One of Batty's inventions. What she does, see, is push you round a jeweller's or some other posh shop and then leaves you near some expensive watches or rings while she goes looking at something else at the other end of the shop, see? Then – snitch, snatch – you help yourself. Of course you'll have to wear a little pixie hat...'

'What?'

'...in case someone peeps inside. And, Sludge, where's Slow's dummy? I told you to fetch it from under 'er pillow.'

''Ere,' said Sludge fishing a huge dummy from the top pocket of her chauffeur's uniform.

'Suck it, Master Plughole, to make you look like a little baby. With the pixie hood over your head and a fluffy quilt wrapped round you, you'll look like a real baby. If anyone comes up and peeps inside just snuggle under the cover and belch at them.'

'Okay.'

'You won't be able to go in the Rolls because Sludge has got to take Miss Delia and Miss Jane out in it soon. Then she'll have to walk round town after them carrying all the stuff they buy and laughin' respectfully at their funny little jokes. So Batty'll drive you into town herself, in the Range Rover.'

'Can't we go in the Jag?'

'No, Master Plug, because the pram wouldn't fit.'

'But where is Batty?'

'Getting dolled up in one of her disguises of course,' explained Granny. 'Here she comes now!'

Chapter 11

'Wow! Sludge – you're a wickedly fast driver!' warbled Delia approvingly. 'But aren't you supposed to stop when the lights are red?'

'Not if you're driving a Rolls,' grunted the chauffeur. Like all bad-tempered people, Sludge enjoyed stamping her feet; that is how she drove the Rolls – in a foot-slam style; she'd slam her foot down onto the accelerator or slam it onto the brake. It made sitting in the back very entertaining. The tyres shrieked, and so did the Blighters.

'You can drop us anywhere near the town centre,' yelped one of the girls as they arrived in Littlebampton, 'then we'll meet you somewhere at 12 o'clock, okay? for you to drive us home for lunch.'

'I thought I 'ad to walk behind you, Miss Jane, carrying parcels,' Sludge muttered in an evil tone; it was as if she didn't approve of girls having servants trotting along behind them to fetch and carry. Something in her voice seemed to imply that the Blighters should follow her about carrying boxes of booze in case she felt thirsty. Sludge always seemed menacing but she must have been smarter than she looked because she could tell which Blighter was talking to her even though she had her back to them. Her ears were huge; maybe that helped.

'You are very welcome to walk behind us if you wish, Sludge,' replied Jane fearlessly, 'but we won't actually be buying anything because we've sort of accidentally run out of pocket money.'

'Well,' exclaimed the chauffeur, 'what are you going into town for?'

'We're going joke-testing,' replied Delia. 'Just a few ideas we've had – like gluing a 10p piece to the floor of a big shop so people keep stopping to try and pick it up...'

'– And we've got these stink bombs, Sludge – you can walk behind us letting them off if you like.'

'No, thank you, Miss Jane. I'll meet you at 12 o'clock like you just said.'

'Where?'

'Outside the Hare and Hounds,' grunted the driver.

'I hope you're not going to drink and drive, Sludge?'

'No, Miss Delia, I'll 've stopped drinking by the time I drive you home.'

'Thank goodness.'

'Drop us here,' cried Jane. Sludge foot-slammed the brake and the Rolls screeched to a sudden stop outside Sainsbury's; the Blighters leapt out, the shop's magic door sprang open and the happy pair piled in looking for mischief.

'It's ages since we tried a SIC,' burbled Jane. 'Let's give it a go.'

The graceful young ladies stopped grinning and looked upwards with startled, serious faces; then they gasped and pointed anxiously at the ceiling. Soon an anxious throng of housewives gathered round and gawped.

'What's the matter?' asked one of them.

'Don't know,' answered another.

'What's everyone looking at?'

The artful twins trickled away leaving a growing group of gaping gawpers.

'Nice one,' chuckled Delia.

'A good start,' agreed Jane. 'Quite the most successful SIC we've ever done.' As I am sure they have taught you at school, SIC stands for Staring Intently at the Ceiling.

'Excuse me,' squeaked Delia politely a few minutes later, 'but haven't you just dropped 10p?' A blonde housewife in dark glasses swept past pushing her pram.

'Goochy – goochy – goo!' she gurgled to her wee babe poking her fluffy, blonde head under the hood to whisper, *I'll park you by the*

booze – Goochy – goochy – goo – *get some whisky and plenty of port* – Give Mummy a ickle smile den diddums – *and a couple of bottles of rum for Granny's chest!*' The baby burped: it was one burp for 'yes' and two for 'no'.

The bouncing blonde flounced past the 10p piece pushing her pram by one hand and towing a trolley with the other. It's awkward trying to shop like that; what mums with prams do is park them in a corner – somewhere where they can keep darting back to keep an eye on them, then they can skip about busily helping themselves with two hands.

The crafty young Blighters waited by the stuck-down coin while the blonde mum parked her lovely babe in a restful corner of the booze section before tripping softly away to the cooked meats where she gazed wistfully at a hunk of ham, then anxiously looked about before she coughed. In his far corner the wee babe heard the all-clear cough; he cautiously poked a long arm through the flap, and nimbly snitched a bottle. Then another.

The lovely mother seemed troubled by a tickle in her throat; she coughed twice as a shopper padded past towards the booze section, then, when the coast was clear, she coughed once more, and the baby's huge fist shot out to clench a bumper bottle of Fine Olde Original MacScrag's Rich, Mellow Scotch Whisky.

'So much for the 10p jape,' sighed Delia on the other side of the shop.

'Total wash out,' moaned Jane.

'Let's go to Laura Ashley's and smear some glue round the rims of a few hats,' suggested Delia thoughtfully, 'so as to liven up people's lives...'

The Blighters surged gracefully out · of Sainsbury's, past the checkouts where a dismounted mounted policeman was talking to the Chief Checkout lady about the Hell's Granny who had swooped the night before, through the magic doors and into the street.

'Hey,' cried Delia, 'what a lovely horse. Look he's tugging at his reins...'

'He wants to follow his master into the shop!'

'He can see the greengroceries in there – I wonder what would happen if we sort of accidentally unhitched him?'

'It would be a kindness.'

'Yes. You're absolutely right. Let's do it!'

The doors sprang open once again and the police horse, Lightning, trotted hungrily towards the greengroceries and started eagerly on the apples. Checkout ladies yelled, but police horses are trained to ignore yelling; it was the sight of his tubby master, Mounted Police Constable Bumsore, that worried him. Lightning whinneyed a worried whinny and trotted off towards the bread; maybe he'd have time to chew a loaf or two of wholemeal before he was caught. A bouncing blonde pranced past pushing a pram; Lightning looked keenly at her head – it looked as if she was balancing a nourishing clump of hay up there. Humans were always giving him hay; that, as far as Lightning was concerned, was what they were for. He'd never before met any that went about with tasty clumps of hay balanced on their heads, but it seemed an excellent idea; more humans should do it. He stretched out his neck, opened his choppers and chomped.

Batty's wig vanished; some of her real hair might have been eaten too had she not leapt away leaving the pram behind to fend for itself. Her dark glasses fell to the floor where Lightning trod on them.

'It's her!' shrieked the Chief Checkout. 'The one that stole the money! I recognise those mad, staring eyes.'

Batty moved swiftly. She took firm hold of Lightning's bridle, swung herself into the saddle and galloped away. The dismounted policeman stood amid the gaping checkout ladies and wondered what to do – but not for long.

'Look at that baby!' yelped the Chief Checkout. 'Working its own pram!'

The pram could be seen attempting to

escape; the ladies could see a baby peering sweetly over the cover – a dear little thing with huge arms which it was using to turn the wheels. The checkout ladies, who were all mums and grannies each with a deep knowledge of babies, were surprised.

'Look at its arms – sticking out like that!'

'It – it's snatching a packet of Mars Bars!'

'And a tin of biscuits!'

'Constable – what are you doing standing there with your mouth open? Arrest that baby!'

Chapter 12

Plughole sat in the pram-scam burping anxiously. Every so often the huge, red face of Constable Bumsore would appear over the top of the cover and peep at him. With a lurch he was wheeled into Littlebampton Police Station.

'What are you doing with that pram?' asked an unseen voice.

'There's a little baby burglar in it, Sergeant.'

BURP!

'So where's its mother?'

'She went galloping off on my horse.'

'I see,' sighed the unseen sergeant, 'so it's been an average sort of morning for you has it, Bumsore?'

'Yes, Sarge.'

A belly appeared in front of the pram and then the portly sergeant peeped inside. His nose shone; his buttons shone; his head shone – and his teeth were shining too (only he'd left them at home, so they shone alone in a smile no one could see). Plughole shrank down amongst the quilting and burped defensively.

'That's wind,' explained Bumsore; he was most knowledgeable about babies – he'd been one himself.

Thrpp!

'So's that.'

'What a hideously ugly-looking baby,' remarked the sergeant as he bent over the pram and squinted in. 'You can tell it's a criminal: I expect it's come from a long line of villains.'

'Long line of gibbons more like,' muttered Bumsore.

'It whiffs a bit,' sniffed the sergeant. 'Maybe you should change its nappy.'

BURPP!!!

'I'm not changing its nappy!'

'Someone's got to look after it.'

'Sloth can,' replied Bumsore firmly. Police Constable Sloth was the third policeman at Littlebampton Police Station, the one that was snoring gently in the next room. His soothing snores seeped under the door as if to lull the baby burglar to slumber.

'Bolt the front door,' ordered the sergeant straightening up; Plughole could only see his stately stomach now – shining with silver buttons. Then it moved away, a pair of hands grabbed the handle and the pram was suddenly wheeled about and pulled into a further room – the one the snores were coming from.

This new room had a fusty, festering scent; Plughole didn't know this, but the smell was mingled of mould, rotting socks, police armpits, stale tobacco, and beer fumes. The young secret agent peeped through the chink where the cover met the side of the hood and watched while the stately sergeant settled comfortably into an easy chair and lifted his magnificent boots onto the table.

PC Sloth, the sleeping policeman, continued to snore gently. The sergeant fished about in the pockets of his tunic and eventually pulled out a pipe.

'This is a sad reflection on modern times, Bumsore,' he sighed nodding in Plughole's direction. 'This is the most juvenile delinquent I have ever met. I blame television.'

'Babies don't watch television.'

'No. But their mothers do. While babies are in their mothers' tummies they absorb criminal influences from programmes like *Grange Hill* and ... er ... '

'*Super Ted?*'

'Exactly. The baby's mother is to blame; I shall tell her so in a minute.'

'But she's galloped off on my horse.'

'She'll be here, Bumsore, just you wait. She'll come here looking for her baby. What

mother could resist the pull on her heart strings of a missing baby?'

'A baby as ugly as that one won't pull no mother's heart strings,' argued PC Bumsore. 'Any young mother would be glad to have got shot of it. Besides, she galloped off and left it in the first place.'

'True,' mused the gleaming sergeant as he puffed thoughtfully. An idea struck him. 'Let's have a look inside that cardboard box,' he suggested. 'Maybe we'll find a clue in there that could lead us to the mother.'

'What cardboard box?'

'The one that's stuffed under the pram. On your feet, Constable, yank it out and put it on the table.'

Chapter 13

'Open up!' cried a voice from the street. 'Open this door or we'll smash it down with our hatchets!'

'Who's that?' asked Bumsore, pausing on his way to investigate the mysterious box.

'Who do you think it is?' sighed the sergeant. 'Who go round with hatchets yelling at people?'

'Red Indians?'

The sergeant sighed again, sucked on his pipe, blew smoke at the ceiling and shook his head. 'It's the Fire Brigade,' he informed Bumsore. 'Go and let them in.'

Plughole heard Bumsore's feet plodding out to the front room, then a new voice was heard in the police station. 'What's the meaning of this?' cried the new voice angrily. 'This sign you stuck on the outside of your front door— *Do not Disturb—in an Emergency Call the Fire Brigade*! You can't stick up notices like that! We're for fires and floods and cats stuck up trees and little boys' heads trapped in railings and people in the bath with their toes stuck up the tap! That's what we're for! Not for police work! Not for something like that!!!'

Plughole could not see the fireman, but he could see the police sergeant turn his head as if looking in a direction that was being pointed at.

'Bring it in here, lads,' cried the fireman. 'Clear the bottles off the table and leave it there!'

Something black and shining suddenly blocked out Plughole's view of the sergeant.

'You can't bring that in here,' he heard him protest. 'Not a coffin!'

'Yes we can. It's lost property – and lost property is *police* business!'

'What do you mean, lost property? How can anyone lose a coffin?'

'Some careless undertaker,' suggested the fireman's voice, 'taking a corner too fast and it's gone flying out the back of his hearse. Something like that must have happened. All I can tell you is that it was found in the street with this on it.'

Plughole didn't see what happened next, but the fireman dropped a wreath over Bumsore's head before leading his team out of the station.

'That's all we need,' groaned the sergeant's voice. 'A baby and a corpse! All right, Constable, go round to the undertaker's and ask if they've mislaid anything. I'll go and sit out front in case anyone comes in to claim it.'

Plughole heard the noise of their boots plodding into the other room, the door closing, and the muffled sound of the sergeant's voice saying, 'Take it off, Bumsore.'

'What?'

'The wreath. Take it off. I know you're dead from the neck up, but there's no need to advertise the fact.'

Then all was quiet. Plughole could hear nothing but PC Sloth's gentle snores. In front of him the polished coffin gleamed. Then, slowly, its top began to open — whatever was inside was lifting the lid.

Chapter 14

The sergeant was idly tuning his police radio to get the Test Match when the door from the street opened and a weeping widow dressed in black staggered sobbing into the station.

'Where is he?' she wailed, dabbing her eyes with an old sock.

'Where is who, madam?'

'Where's my Albert?'

'Albert?'

'He fell off the roof-rack,' croaked the crone. 'They never tied him down proper.'

'This Albert, madam, would he be dead by any chance? Would he be a deceased person?'

'Yes,' wailed the widow, 'we was taking him to the taxidermist.'

'You were, were you?' said the sergeant using his deeply sympathetic voice.

'And he came off of the roof,' sobbed the grieving gran. 'I was going to bury him; that's why I got the coffin and the spade, then...then I thought 'e wouldn't like it – not all them worms gnawing at him. So I thought I'd take him down the whatsitsname and have him cremated and sprinkle his ashes round his beloved places – pubs and betting shops and the amusement arcade – but then...*sob*...then I thought *'e won't like that neither* – 'e never liked it hot, see, he'd come out in a rash...so then I thought I'll have him stuffed and sit him in front of the telly. It'd be just like he'd never died – he weren't talkative, not Albert. So I rings the taxidermist and says, *Can you do him in a sitting position with the features sort of sadly smiling?* And he says, *No problems,* he says, *bring 'im round. Do you want him cross-legged? and which was the feature you wanted sadly smiling?* Only when we got there he'd fallen off.'

The kindly sergeant, using his deeply sympathetic voice and manner, helped the old lady and her brave daughters with Albert's coffin. 'It ain't half heavy,' he grunted.

'Yeh,' said one of the daughters, 'that'll be the booze.'

'He was a martyr to it,' growled the other daughter quickly.

'It swole him up something chronic,' sobbed the granny. 'He'll take an awful lot of stuffing – unless I get him done thinner. What do you think, girls? They could take a tuck in and it'd save on materials.'

This time they tied the coffin firmly and, wailing like a bagpipe, the grieving gran slumped into her Range Rover where she was revived with brandy. It took a lot of it before

she felt better, then she blew her nose into the sock and handed it to the sergeant. 'Thank you, Officer,' she sniffed. 'Drive on, my dear,' she said to the rugged daughter at the wheel.

'Well,' smiled the sergeant, 'that's got shot of Albert. Now for the cardboard box!' He strode into the inner room in his beautiful boots and peeped into the pram.

It was empty. The infant criminal had disappeared.

Chapter 15

The whirling, swirling sound of merry laughter from inside a coffin is rarely heard nowadays.

'Put a sock in it, Master Plug, or you'll 'ave your cousins comin' to see what's up.' croaked Granny as she opened up the lid. The Range Rover was safely back in the garage and Granny, Sludge and Slow had hoisted the coffin to the floor.

'He's been laughing fit to bust all the way back,' cackled little Batty, as she clambered nimbly out of the coffin.

'See, it was all them bottles what made it so heavy,' remarked Slow.

'Take 'em to the kitchen,' barked Granny, 'I'll drink 'em for me tea.'

'But I thought we had to store loot and never spend it or damage it,' cried Plughole.

'Yes, well, that is...er...partly true,' replied the Chief Inspector. But in my case, with a weak chest, I am allowed the odd crate of stolen booze to lubricate my tubes.'

'I see.'

'Come on! Come on!' snapped the Chief. 'Don't just stand there—let's get out of these disguises and back under cover.'

'Under cover?' asked Plughole.

'Yes. We are undercover agents, aren't we? We got to pretend to be servants again.'

'Tell you what, Plughole,' suggested Batty as they trickled into the kitchens, 'you could go for a ride on that horse. I got him parked in the old stable – very gentle he is. It won't do no harm, Granny, for the boy to have a bit of a ride round on it.'

'It's nearly two o'clock,' was the reply, 'and we haven't served up lunch yet. Get out of them baby clothes, Master Plug, then come to my kitchen and I'll give you a sandwich before you go for your ride.'

'Okay.'

'Gawd knows what your cousins are doing,' she grumbled. ''Ere,' she shoved a roll stuffed with what looked like chicken into the lad's hand. 'Go and find Batty's 'orse.' The eager lad loped off.

'Sludge!' yelled Granny. 'Go and find them girls and tell 'em their luncheon is getting cold.'

'I thought it was frog salad followed by squirrel vomit sorbet,' grumbled Sludge.

'Well, tell 'em it's getting warm.'

Sludge stomped off to hunt for the Blighters; she trudged to the library and then to the music room.

'Serves 'em right if they starve,' she grumbled.

The Blighters were high up at the top of the house in Plughole's attic. He had an attic, you see, instead of a bedroom and an old travelling trunk instead of a bed. The Blighters had thoughtfully crept into the lad's attic in order to leave a glass of water and a nourishing chocolate biscuit on the cardboard box by his trunk. He had a trunkside box, you see, instead of a bedside table. The biscuit was made of rubber, of course, and the glass was stuck down so that he'd lift up the bedside box when he tried to drink it.

'Pity we can't give him an apple-pie bed,' sighed Delia. 'But you need sheets for that.'

'We could tie knots in his pyjamas,' suggested Jane.

'Yes. He'd enjoy that. We'd hear him laugh his laugh in the still of the night.'

'He's a really nice kid,' mused Jane thoughtfully, 'with a wondrous laugh. It's a sort of gift, a laugh like that. A God-given gift.'

'It certainly is,' agreed her sister. 'We'll take care of Plughole when we grow up.'

'We can give him a job in our joke factory!'

'Yes. He could have a highly skilled job — testing farting powder!' There was a pause in

74

the conversation while the Blighters had hysterics. Then one of them continued (I think it was Jane). 'Testing farting powder would be a very good job for Plughole.'

'Yes,' agreed the other one, 'the sort of job you don't have to pass exams for!'

'Or if you do – then they'd be purely practical – like music exams!'

Conversation lapsed once again. Eventually Jane wiped her tears away and turned to her sister wearing the solemn expression of one who wishes to change the subject to something serious. 'I think, Delia, that it's time we tried a jape or two on those wretched dinner ladies to serve them right for letting us starve.'

'Yah,' agreed Delia poshly. 'High time they were taught a firm lesson.'

'We have been far too lax,' burbled Jane. 'It's quite wrong that someone as revolting as Sludge should not have her life plagued and harassed. I bet she's got sheets on *her* bed – let's go and take a look!'

But all the servants' rooms were locked. 'Never fear,' smiled Delia, 'we can get a ladder out, sneak in at the windows, make a few apple-pie beds...'

'Sew up the odd pair of tights...'

'Yah!'

'Put itching powder in their knickers...'

'And a plastic dog turd on Slow's pillow!'

The first window the girls climbed in at was Batty's.

'Good grief,' burbled a Blighter. 'Dozens of wigs! Look, a couple of Dolly Parton wigs – like that peculiar woman had on in Sainsbury's. Look, they're all labelled – *Dolly Parton*, *Dame Edna*, a *Funky* wig, a *St. Trinian's*, a *Max Wall*. Cor! You must try this one.'

'A *Whacko Jacko*. Does it suit me?'

'Absolutely!'

'Hey! Look! Disguises! Would you believe it – she's got dozens of *noses* all neatly sorted into rows. Wow – plastic bottoms too, with tie-on tapes!'

'What are these? Moustaches!'

'Not to mention beards...'

'Try this one, it'll match the *Whacko Jacko*...'

'I just love these hats...'

'Cor! Masks! A Prince Charles and a Madonna and...'

'Look, she's tons of make-up. And here's a hairy wart – most useful!'

'What's she got in this sack – hey look, loadsa money – great bundles of £20 notes!'

'Jane,' said Delia suddenly serious, 'do you know what I think?'

'Yes,' replied Jane. 'You think our dear

mother's marvellous new staff are *not* really
servants at all. You think they are just
pretending and all the time they are really a
fiendish gang of...'

But Jane never finished that interesting
sentence because, from the door, came the
unmistakable sound of a key being turned in
the lock. The Blighters turned and fled to the
window – but their ladder had gone.

'Lookin' for something?' croaked a deadly
voice.

Chapter 16

'Here is your luncheon, madam,' said Batty respectfully as she placed the silver tray on Amelia Blight's bed.

'Thank you, Batty; it smells good, what is it?'

'Ratatouille,' replied the little lady's maid graciously. She nearly went on to say that she'd help Granny catch the rat, but managed to stay respectfully silent.

'You can spoon it into my mouth,' said Amelia Blight, 'to save me the trouble.'

'Very good, madam.'

'As a matter of fact I want to ask your advice about the book I'm writing — *Belinda Batt Goes to Smuggler's Cove* — I'm on Chapter 10 and Belinda Batt and her cousins are camping out on Muckdrood Moor in their dear little tents and drinking gallons of cocoa prepared by Henrietta...'

'Ate who, madam?'

'Henrietta, Batty, it's a name.'

'I thought you said *Henry ate her*, madam.'

The great writer sighed. 'Henrietta is one of Belinda Batt's cousins. He's a little boy that's really called Henry but he wishes he was a

little girl so he calls himself Henrietta and wears a pink frock. Don't you think that's sweet?'

'Yes, madam,' replied Batty skilfully spooning a tender chunk of rat into the Blight's fat face.

'Well,' chewed the Blight, 'the children see lights out to sea – signalling – and a boat-load of smugglers row ashore and find Henrietta and capture the poor little chap and poke fun at him; what I want your advice about is what should happen next. Often the ideas of ordinary people, like yourself, can be useful to a creative person like me. So – what would you suggest?'

'Well, madam,' replied Batty quietly, 'the smugglers could do the same as Granny's going to do with the young ladies...'

'What *do* you mean?'

'Miss Delia, madam, and Miss Jane – Granny caught 'em nicking stuff from my collection, madam...'

'What collection?'

'My disguise collection, madam. So she went in with her blunderbuss and...'

'Wait a minute, Batty, what exactly is a blunderbuss? It sounds like a bus going in the wrong direction.'

'A blunderbuss, madam,' replied Batty still spooning grub into the Blight's face, 'is a sort of gun, madam. It shoots shot.'

'Shoots shot!' cried Amelia Blight white with fright. Her chubby chops were trembling.

'Yes, madam, it shoots shot in all directions. It is used, madam, by elderly armed robbers – on account of them not being so keen-sighted, madam, as the younger ones – so, with a blunderbuss, they're more likely to hit what they're aiming at. Only, madam, they often hit all sorts of other things besides. Sludge and Slow, madam, have often been shot in the bum. You have to keep well back, madam, when Granny's got her blunderbuss out.'

'Are you telling me that Fang is an armed robber?'

'She don't do it so often nowadays, madam, because you've got to be nimble on your pins for armed robbery. She's more into sedentary crime nowadays.'

'Sedentary crime?'

'Yes, madam, where the criminal just lolls about and the victims bring them money. Like kidnapping rich kids, madam, whose mothers wouldn't like them to come to no harm.'

'Oh Batty,' wailed the Blight. 'What is that woman going to do to my darlings?'

'She's going to play pooh-sticks with them, madam.'

'Pooh-sticks?'

'It's a game, madam, invented by Pooh, madam, and Piglet. In a book, madam, which you never wrote, madam, and this book gave Granny the idea of what to do with the twins, madam.'

'What do you mean?' gasped the Blight faintly.

'She's got 'em tied up in sacks, madam,

and she's going to drop 'em both into the water, madam, at exactly the same time, and the one that drowns last is the winner.'

Amelia Blight stared at Batty in disbelief. The little lady's maid was so neat and humble it was difficult to believe she was a crook. 'Of course, madam, if you want me to *plead* with Granny I will, madam.'

'You could plead with her?'

'Yes, madam, but if Granny was to be pleaded with it would help if I was to be able to say to her that you was anxious to give her a little gift, madam.'

'Like a box of chocolates?'

'A box would do very well, madam, but not chocolates.'

'No chocolates?'

'No, madam. Money, madam. That is what it would take to stop Granny having her revenge on them girls for them nicking wigs and beards and stuff and being stuck-up little madams, madam – a million pounds in used notes tied up in a box with a ribbon.'

'A ribbon?'

'A nice pink ribbon, madam. That should do the trick. One million pounds by midnight – or Miss Jane and Miss Delia go for THE BIG SPLASH!'

Chapter 17

Sergeant Slipper put down the telephone, gave it a quick dusting with his hankie and spoke. 'Your horse has been sighted, Bumsore.'

'Where?' replied the constable turning his rich red face towards the gleaming one.

'The first sighting was in the Nag's Head Public House in Little Dribbling,' explained the trusty sergeant. 'He trotted in through the front door and out the back into the beer garden where he browsed for a while on the landlord's roses before he jumped over the hedge.'

Bumsore nodded his huge head, and the gleaming one continued. 'He was next seen upstairs in a hat shop in Firkinford.'

'I didn't know there was a hat shop in Firkinford.'

'There isn't. Not any more.'

'Well, Sarge, he'll come home when he's hungry.'

'That may not be for some time, Bumsore. He's eaten all the hats – not to mention the roses and God knows what else. Besides, there's some horrible, little yob on his back egging him on and laughing an evil laugh...probably the son of the woman that stole the horse in the first pláce.'

'The brother of the little baby burglar?'

'Exactly. What a family!'

Even though Plughole had been brought up in a circus and was used to riding, the horse Lightning tended to ignore the little lad and trotted about at will wherever he wished — which was usually in the direction of food. After the refreshing feast of roses and hats, he ambled into a pleasant meadow where he paused to crop the lush grass.

Plughole gave up trying to get Lightning to move and, fishing in his pocket, re-read a letter that he had received a week before. It was grubby and dog-eared because he took it about with him in the back pocket of his jeans.

Before you read it I should explain that Plughole's real name was Peter. That was what his mum and dad called him, especially when they were being serious, and, as you will see, although Plug's dad was a clown, his letter to his little son was serious and sad:

H.M. PRISON – DARTMOOR
Dear Peter,
How are you, old chap? All right, Dad, I

hear you say. Well then, why was your letter so smudged? Was it raining when you wrote it? Son – don't be afraid to tell us if you are lonely or if your aunty isn't kind to you. Don't keep it bottled up – you might go off pop!

Remember this – one day your mum and me will be proved innocent. We'll be let out and we'll come for you and the family will be together again. You may think that this is hard to believe, but don't despair. What will we do, Pete, when we come down and fetch you? Shall we go back to a circus or try some other lark?

Tell me what you think.

All my love,

Dad

A little drop – maybe it was rain – fell onto the clown's crumpled letter. Then the boy folded it carefully and replaced it in the back pocket of his jeans.

It was many hours later, when night had fallen and owls, moths, bats and the moon were out, that an exhausted Plughole staggered up the posh steps that led to the front doors of Blight Hall. They were swinging open, you see, so, even though he was supposed to come in through the kitchens, Plug trickled up those steps and sneaked straight into the posh part of the house. He closed the heavy doors behind him, then listened; the house was deathly silent; moonbeams seeped softly through elegant windows making the silence spooky. Hastily the boy stretched out a hand and snapped on the light – the hall was bare; no pictures of grand ladies or fine gentlemen were left on the walls; suits of armour no longer stood stiffly by the stairs. Where was the priceless Persian carpet? Where were the silver candlesticks?

Plughole's feet echoed emptily from room to room. What had happened? Where was everybody? Even the kitchens were deserted; no friendly Fang or cheery Batty; no bumbling Slow or grumpy Sludge. The doors of Granny's booze cupboard hung open revealing empty shelves.

But at least there was plenty of food left in the fridges and freezers. Remember that Plughole had only had a frog roll since breakfast – and it had been a fairly eventful day for the young secret agent of police: pram-scamming, burping, being arrested, escaping, riding through hat shops, destroying a flower show, joining the jousting at Piddleford Tournament, coming first in the Blightminster

Donkey Derby, being disqualified, protesting, trotting off disdainfully, galloping towards the stables of Littlebampton Police Station at feeding time, scrambling off just in time, and jogging four miles home – all this makes a boy peckish.

Plughole poured himself a glass of milk. Then another. He staggered to the soda stream and mixed himself a Coke. He ate a modest slab of chocolate ice-cream, a cold sausage roll – while another two were in the oven – a hot sausage roll; a burnt sausage roll; a tin of peaches; two slices of toast; six cream crackers; a tin of condensed milk; then he burped – just like the baby burglar.

'Who's there?' wailed a frail wail; his aunt peered nervously round the kitchen door. 'Oh, Plughole, it's only you.'

'What's been going on?' asked the weary boy. 'Where are the twins and the servants? Why has all the good furniture and the piano and everything gone?'

'Oh Plughole,' wailed the Blight, tears cascading down her chubby cheeks like rain down a pig's bottom. 'Something terrible has happened!'

Chapter 18

'I've sold everything I possibly could,' explained Aunt Amelia as she sat at the kitchen table, 'my jewels, my watch, the pictures, the cars, everything. And I've been to the bank and got a loan, which means I'll eventually have to sell the house in order to pay it all back.'

'So you've got the million pounds?' asked Plughole amazed.

'Yes. In used notes just like Batty said. It's in this suitcase – tied up with a pink ribbon.' She lifted it onto the table.

'Did the bank have that much?' asked Plughole.

'No, they didn't. They had to ring London and arrange for a security van to bring it to the house. It only came about half an hour ago; I was getting terribly worried. Look!' She opened the suitcase lid for Plug to see the cash then she snapped the catches shut again. 'How long have we got, Plughole, what's the time?'

'Five past eleven,' replied the boy.

Amelia Blight sighed. She had been working frantically to collect the cash ever since Batty had named the sum. Now that it was all ready she had nothing to do to stop her worrying about the Blighters. 'The money's okay,' she continued, 'but how do I know they'll really give back the girls? They could just barge in, couldn't they, with their frightful blunderbuss shooting shot...'

'Shooting shot, Aunt Amelia?'

'That is what it does, Plughole. They could simply swipe the money, drive away and...and still play pooh-sticks with my darlings.'

'Pooh-sticks, Aunt?'

'Yes, Plughole. Stop interrupting me. I keep wondering whether I was wise not to tell the police. But Batty said they'd know as soon as I made any sort of contact with them and...and the girls would be pushed in – in sacks...' She had to stop talking in order to blow her nose and dab her streaming eyes with a hanky. Even though she'd been such a pain to him, Plughole gave her a reassuring hug. 'Don't worry, Aunt Amelia. I'm sure that Batty really expected you to call the police station. That would be why they kidnapped the girls.'

'What are you talking about, Plughole?'

'The servants aren't really criminals. They're just pretending. You see they are really a very high-up team of police agents from Scotland Yard sent to test the Littlebampton police.'

'You're crazy, Plughole. You are raving like a loon!'

'No, honestly, it's true. They told me after I heard them talking about Batty snatching cash from Sainsbury's. They're sent all round the country by Scotland Yard to test out local police stations – 'specially if they are believed to be slack like ours are. They commit crimes, you see, Aunt, and then see how long it takes for the local police to catch them. Batty...'

'You foolish child,' snapped the Blight, 'Scotland Yard wouldn't send police officers about the country kidnapping children!'

Plughole thought about this, and kept his wide mouth shut.

'No, they are criminals all right,' his aunt declared. 'Batty boasted about it quite openly; they used to be armed robbers but now they're trying more artful dodges, that's what she said. They go round schools disguised as dinner ladies and go out house-breaking in the evenings. That's what they were doing here except that the twins broke into Batty's room and discovered their disguises and their loot – so they kidnapped them to serve them right.'

'But how would they know if you did ring the police?'

'I'm not going to risk it,' replied the Blight firmly. 'They must be out there somewhere.' She waved a ringless hand at the kitchen window. 'They might have the phone tapped...'

'Tapped?'

'Yes. Granny Fang could be out there somewhere under a telegraph pole with a pair of ear-phones on. Honestly, Plughole, I'd rather lose the money than risk telling the police. What's the time?'

'Eleven fifteen.'

'Oh, Plughole, when I give them the money they might just clear off with it without letting the girls go. They might have drowned them already for all we know.'

'But, Aunt Amelia, you're always writing adventure stories, can't you think up a plan?'

'My head's in a spin, Plughole. I can't think at all.'

'But have you ever written about anyone being kidnapped?'

'Yes,' replied the writer with a frown of concentration. 'In *Alice Challis and the Perilous Palace*, Alice gets kidnapped by spies because her dad, Harris Challis, is a scientist who's invented this secret formula which these spies want, you see, so they kidnap Alice Challis and keep her in this palace. Then they tell her dad that they'll toss her into this pit of asps . . . '

'Asps?'

'They're snakes, Plughole. Deadly ones. They threaten to throw her into this pit writhing with evil asps unless the dad gives them the secret formula.'

'And did he?'

'He was very cool and cunning, Plughole, and marvellously clever, which is what one would expect of Harris Challis, or any other top scientist; he quickly wrote out another secret formula which looked exactly like the real one but wasn't, see? And the spies, being foreign, fell for it and swapped Alice for the dud plans.'

'You could do something like that,' cried Plughole. He almost laughed he was so excited.

'But they don't want a secret formula,' wailed the Blight bitterly. 'They want this.' She banged a fist onto the suitcase. 'And they are not going to get it until those girls are absolutely safe. I think I'll hide the suitcase somewhere . . . What's that?'

'The telephone.'

'What's the time?'

'Eleven twenty-five.'

'Bring the suitcase,' she yelled as she dashed

towards the ringing. 'Don't let it out of your sight!' So saying the Blight beetled off.

'Blight Hall,' she whispered tremblingly as she lifted the receiver.

'Good evening, madam,' chuckled a throaty voice. 'I've got a young lady that wants a word with you...'

'Mum!' yelped a nervous Blighter. 'It's me, Delia.'

'Are...are you all right, my angel, they...they haven't drowned your sister, have they?'

'Not yet,' was the grim answer. 'We're both as all right as it's possible to be if you've been kept in a sack all day without food or...ouch!'

'Listen,' croaked Fang's deadly voice. 'We're coming to the house at midnight as arranged. Have you got the money?'

'Yes. But how will I know you'll give me back my girls?'

There was laughter at the other end of the phone. Granny could be heard telling the others. Then Batty's merry cackle cried, 'You'll have to trust us, madam, after all we are your loyal servants – aren't we!' There was more laughter; then the phone was slammed down.

'Oh, Plughole, it was them,' wailed Amelia Blight. 'Plughole, where are you?'

But Plughole was nowhere to be seen. And neither was the suitcase.

Amelia Blight stood alone by the phone in the empty hall and howled. She hardly noticed when the lights suddenly went out, but when she heard the sound of approaching motor-bikes, she pulled herself together and waddled over to stand in front of the great fireplace so as to look important.

The roar of engines ceased and, moments

later, three grim figures in horned helmets loped into the great hall.

'What?' chortled Batty when Amelia Blight had explained about the money. 'You mean little Plughole has nicked the million quid?'

'Oh dear,' grinned Granny sharkishly in the eerie moonlight, 'so it's pooh-sticks time, is it?'

'No!' screamed Amelia Blight. 'Let me see my children.'

'Shurrup! Sludge, watch 'er. If she does anything foolish tap her on the napper. Batty, you and I'll search for Master Plughole, call for him – kindly now – remember he's *one of us* (or thinks he is). Master Plughole, Plug'ole my boy, come out and see your pals!'

'Where are you, Plug? Did you 'ave a nice ride on the horse? Come on, where are you hiding?' called Batty sweetly.

'Here I am, Inspector Batty,' cried an eager voice from the stairs. The heroic boy bounced trippingly down to the hall clutching a bulging suitcase firmly tied with pink ribbon.

'And you've got the cash?' croaked Granny.

'Yes. I thought it my duty to take charge of it, Chief. Aunt Amelia was having doubts about giving it to you – she was going to hide it.'

'Good lad. Now, say "Goodbye" to your aunt and we'll go and find your cousins. With

97

luck Slow won't have dropped 'em down the mineshaft yet. Mark you, we told 'er to do it if we weren't back in an hour.'

'You've not been here long.'

'I know. But now I think about it, Slow never learnt to tell the time properly. Let's hope we ain't too late. But, whatever happens, you done well, Plug. I shall recommend you for a medal.'

Chapter 19

It was frightening racing through the moonlight on the back of Batty's motor-bike. She kept turning her horned head to cackle merrily at the anxious boy, but he could never hear what she was yelling above the revving engine's roar. Once they'd turned off the road and were speeding over the moorland, Plughole felt safer; there was no longer any fear of oncoming traffic and, anyway, crashing into heather and gorse didn't seem so bad. The moon bathed the moor in a silvery light strong enough to throw romantic shadows of racing riders in horned helmets behind them. It was a bleak and windswept place with crags, nags, and bleating sheep which roamed about nibbling sparse grass and dropping droppings. By day the deadly buzzard sailed overhead; at night the mousing owl swooped. No one lived there, but, about one hundred years ago, there had been many mines upon the moor. Miners had come out from far villages every day singing *Hey Ho, Hey Ho, It's off to work we go* and dug mineshafts here and there amid the sparse grass. These huge holes were still there; if you were to drop a stone

down one, you could count to ten before you'd hear the splash.

As you see, it was dangerous to saunter about the moor by night in case you dropped down a huge hole, but the gang kept to the track and rode in line rather than the V-formation which, as you know, is usual with dinner ladies.

After about five miles down the moorland track, they came across Amelia Blight's stolen Rolls parked close to one of the deadly mineshafts. A makeshift tent made of string, sticks and sheets of polythene flapped emptily and, beside the embers of a camp fire, Slow sat talking to a pair of sacks.

'It's no good sulking,' she was saying. 'Granny and the others have come back. That was their bikes you heard. If they didn't get the money they are gonna chuck you both down the 'ole. Or was they gonna chuck you down if they did get the money? What was it, Miss Jane?'

Miss Jane ignored the dimmest dinner lady and her sack remained silent and aloof.

'Lost your tongue, have you?' grumbled Slow. 'You was chattering away just now...'

'Don't be daft, Slow,' hissed Sludge who had darted away from Granny and Batty and sneaked over to where Slow was nattering to the Blighters.

'They're gagged, aren't they? They can't talk to you.'

'Did Madam give Granny the million quid?' asked Slow happily. 'Can I buy myself a little dolly and some sweeties and a monkey?'

''Course you can,' nodded Sludge, then a fierce frown twisted her hard face. 'That is, if we ever get our share; I don't trust Batty and Granny—look at 'em over there whisperin' to each other. They could scarper with the lot and leave us with nothing. They was always very thick, them two.'

'I thought I was the one what was thick.'

'You are thick—meaning stupid, but Granny and Batty are thick meaning thick as thieves, see?'

'No.'

'Well, it means they like each other and don't like us, see? They use us to do their dirty work but grudge giving us our proper shares. That's what I'm saying.'

Slow squinted across the camp to where Batty and Granny were muttering to each other. She stepped up close to one of Sludge's enormous lugholes and, after a long period of deep thought, she whispered, 'We could steal the money off of Granny.'

'Yes, Slow, we could. In fact that is exactly

what we will do. Stay 'ere and watch me out the corner of your eye. I'm going to nobble the bikes so they can't come after us.'

'Nobble?'

'Yeh. I'll pull the leads to the sparking plugs off of 'em and chuck 'em into the bracken. Then, when I've done 'em all, you'll see me walk calmly towards Granny and, for a sign I'll blow my nose. Understand. Soon as you see me do that you must create a diversion...'

'A what?'

'Soon as you see me blow my nose, then you must pick up these sacks...'

'What? Miss Delia and Miss Jane?'

'Yes. Pick 'em up and heave them down the mineshaft. That'll make Granny and Batty come running to look what you done, see? They'll look down the 'ole and say things like, "It can't be helped," and "Never mind," and "It's no good crying over spilt milk." And while they're doing that I pick up the suitcase and climb into the Rolls and you, Slow, come trotting over and get in beside me. Then we drive away with the lot!'

'A whole million pounds!'

'Yeh. And you will get half. Now, watch carefully for me to give the sign.'

'Okay.'

On the other side of the camp site, young Plughole plucked up his courage and interrupted Granny. 'Will you be letting Delia and Jane go now, Chief?' the young agent asked anxiously.

'No,' croaked Granny. 'I reckon your aunt's good for another million. What do you think, Inspector Batty?'

'I believe you're right,' cackled Inspector Batty cheerfully. 'She raised the first million so quick she's bound to be able to get hold of another if we give her a couple of days and put the frighteners on 'er. Where's your blunderbuss, Granny? I'll let the girls out their sacks for a bit so that they can have a drink...' The sudden sound of two deep splashes interrupted her.

'Blimey!' groaned Granny. 'That idiot Slow has dropped 'em down the 'ole!'

'Well,' observed Batty dryly. 'They won't need no drinks now!'

'No,' agreed Granny. 'The last thing they'll be down there is thirsty.'

Chapter 20

Sludge slammed her foot onto the accelerator and shot down the track towards the road. Of course she had not waited for Slow, simply nabbed the loot, jumped into the Rolls, and buzzed off as soon as Batty and Granny had arrived at the mineshaft.

As you know, Sludge seldom smiled but frowned forever fiercely but she was grinning now as she sped down the moonlit track. It was high time, she told herself, that she split from the Fang Gang; Batty and Granny could not be trusted; besides, she, Sludge, should have been the leader – but Batty always sided with Granny Fang and Slow was too thick to be much help.

'Granny's very strong on revenge,' thought the Sludge. 'She'll come looking for me with her blunderbuss. And Batty is packed with guile, she'll sniff me out.' This was true, Batty had been trained at the Royal College of Burglary and was, without doubt, the most artful crook in England. 'I'll phone the police when I get to Litlebampton,' planned Sludge, 'and tell 'em exactly where the other three are and how they've drowned a couple of innocent kids. That way they'll be arrested for murder. Then I'll be completely safe!' She turned off the moorland track onto the road and, a few minutes later, pulled up beside a public phone box in the sleeping town of Littlebampton.

Sergeant Slipper took a very long time to answer the phone. 'Do you realise what time it is?' he snapped. 'It's three o'clock in the morning! We're all in bed catching up on our beauty sleep; we've had a very busy day! Ring the Fire Brigade!'

Sludge slammed the receiver down, picked it up again and dialled 999 for the second time. It did not take long for her to inform the Fire Brigade that two children tied up in sacks had been dropped down a mineshaft out on the moor and that the three arch-criminals that had done it were stranded there. Then she hung up once again and bounded back to the purring Rolls.

Her plan was simple; drive to London and start spending money. First she'd get herself a facelift so as to look even more beautiful – just a few minor alterations, nothing drastic – new ears, a new nose, a new chin, and a new pair of eyes. Next she'd sign on at a posh health farm and eat prunes and carrots until she was thin, then she'd splash out on clothes and jewels; maybe she'd buy herself a house or two and hire a lady's maid and a cook—real ones. She'd always wanted a racehorse and a yacht.

Sludge grinned again. It was getting to be a habit.

As soon as Sludge had driven off with the loot, Batty had smelt danger.

'She's ripped the plug leads off of the bikes,' reported Granny.

'What would you do, Granny, if you was Sludge and had just double-crossed us and left us stranded in the middle of a miserable moor miles from anywhere with a couple of drowned brats on our hands?'

'I'd tip off the cops,' croaked the crone thoughtfully, 'and hope they'd round us up so that we wouldn't come after her.'

'Yes. That's what she'll do. She's not smart enough to be a true artist, Sludge ain't, but she's just artful enough to think of that.'

'We'll get done for murder if they catch us,' growled Granny. 'Slow, what did you want to throw them girls in for?'

'Sludge told me to,' answered Slow. 'She was going to give me half the money. But she left me behind.'

'You've been had for a sucker, Slow,' snapped Granny angrily. 'Think yourself lucky you're my own sister's child or I'd shoot you this minute and chuck you in after them. In fact I think I'll do that anyway. Batty, fetch us my gun!'

'I've got a better idea,' whispered Batty winking in the moonlight. 'Slow,' she called, 'do you want Granny to shoot you?'

Slow thought for a minute. 'No,' she replied.

'Well, what you've got to do, Slow, if you want to get back into Granny's good books, is wait here by the mineshaft...'

'What? The big hole?'

'Yeh. Wait beside it and when the coppers come, tell 'em what you done and tell 'em it was Sludge told you to do it, see? And say Granny and me jumped down the hole to try to save them. Got that?'

'Yeh.'

'Good girl. What are you going to tell them?'

'I'm going to say I threw them posh girls down the hole in sacks because Sludge told me to and you and Granny jumped in after them to try to save 'em.'

'Very good, Slow,' chuckled Granny. 'We jumped down after 'em, bravely, see? And never come up again. Understand?'

'Yeh.'

'Right, Master Plughole,' croaked the gang leader turning to the bewildered boy who stood trembling in the moonlight, tears oozing from his eyes. 'Batty and me are making a break across the moor – and you're coming with us. You're our insurance policy.'

Plughole staggered along between the two queens of crime as they cut away from the track down a path between high bracken. He vaguely understood what Granny Fang had meant by the term *insurance policy* – that if the police looked like catching them, they'd threaten to shoot him. People always said that young Plughole, although a perky little chap with a gladsome bath laugh, was not one of the world's great brains. His cousins, for example, the late Miss Delia and the late Miss Jane, had firmly believed that the only exam Plug could ever pass would have to be purely practical – remember?

What do you think about Plughole's brain?

I see.

Well, you are absolutely right. In fact Plughole had twigged that the dinner ladies were not really police agents when his aunt had wailed at him about Scotland Yard not sending police officers about the country kidnapping kids; he'd suddenly seen that what she was wailing was true. He'd realised how he had been artfully tricked and cunningly duped into helping them commit crime. Then he had pondered deeply on what his aunt had wailed about the dinner ladies not necessarily giving back the girls after they got the money. That is when he had decided to pretend he still believed that they were secret agents of police and to go back with them to their lair to see if he could rescue the Blighters.

Maybe that wasn't very bright, but, you have to agree, it was brave. But Plughole had failed. His cousins had gone for the big splash; what is more he had been a witness of the murder; Granny and Batty would have guessed that he no longer believed that they were simply going about testing the police. They'd use him as an *insurance policy* during their escape, but if they succeeded and got off the moor without being seen, then what would they do to him?

Plughole tramped along between the crooks weeping softly. He kept telling himself that the smartest thing he could do would be to dodge away into the bracken. But what about Granny's gun. And what if he were to run slap into another mineshaft?

Did it matter? Delia and Jane were dead — the only people apart from his mum and dad that had loved him and appreciated his talents. They had been older than him, and had gone to the poshest girls' school in the country, but they hadn't bossed him about or looked down on him; they'd always been his friends. They'd been going to look after him when they were grown-ups and had cheered him up with their special scheme for dealing with life — which was to look on the bright side and have a good laugh.

'It's no good having a laugh like yours, Plug, and not using it all the time,' they used to say.

Maybe he should just take a chance and run, Plughole was thinking madly and sadly when he saw something luminous shining ahead of them.

'What's that?' barked Granny.

'Ghosts!' hissed Batty.

She was right; ghosts were watching them from a little hillock about twenty metres up the path. The awful thing about ghosts is the way they look at you with dead eyes.

Then one of them spoke.

Chapter 21

'Go away!' screamed Granny. 'Or I'll shoot the boy!' Plughole felt cold metal press into his neck. He thought of Granny's finger on the trigger. What if she twitched with fright?

The ghosts stood a little way off on their hillock watching. Strangely you could see them more clearly when the moon went behind a black cloud. The two of them shone out and Plughole could see their shining mouths move as they whispered to each other. Then one of them turned towards Granny and answered, 'If you shoot him, we will follow you wherever you go...'

'We will tell the police where to find you...' wailed the other ghost.

'Just let that valuable boy go...'

'Fancy threatening to shoot Plughole, a most talented laugher.'

'A boy with a bright future...'

'Provided he passes his exams...'

'I'm sure he will,' wailed the late Miss Delia, 'they'll be purely practical...'

'And he's had plenty of practice,' agreed the late Miss Jane.

'It weren't us what drowned you,' screamed

Batty. 'It was Sludge and Slow. We're innocent!'

'Let that boy go,' yelled the Jane ghost.

'Or we will haunt you for ever,' called Delia.

Plughole felt a sudden shove in his back as Granny pushed him forward towards the ghosts on their hillock. He fell on sparse grass and some prickles; when he sat up Batty and Granny had gone.

'Let's chase after them,' suggested one of his dead cousins when the Blighters arrived. Plughole thought it was Delia but it was difficult to tell.

'No,' cried Plughole. 'Let them go. They might shoot me!'

'Good heavens, Plughole,' cried Jane, 'where's your sense of adventure? Think of the sheer bliss of seeing Granny Fang wet herself with fear.'

'Can't we just go and find help?' suggested the crumpled boy.

'Honestly, Plughole,' said the Delia ghost, 'it's tragic to hear your woeful witterings. A young lad should always find time for a wheeze. Is this the Plughole whom we have trained to laugh in face of danger?'

'The Plughole who is going to be a clown when he grows up?'

'And a daredevil tester of farting powder!'

'How can someone as brave and romantic as that go all feeble about a teeny little risk of getting shot?'

As you see, being rescued by the Blighters was almost as bad as being captured by the dinner ladies!

'I say,' said Jane, 'isn't that dawn coming up in the east, how picturesque.'

'Don't ghosts go back to their graveyards at dawn?' asked Plughole faintly. He was torn, you see, between love and fear – he didn't want his dead cousins to leave him, but it was scary talking to them as they shone eerily beside him.

'Normally yes, Plughole, but we don't actually have a graveyard yet. Our bodies have yet to be discovered, so we will linger on and keep an eye on you.'

'We'll guard you from passing dinner ladies,' explained Delia. 'And guide you back to the track and help you find the road and make sure you turn in the right direction to get to Littlebampton.'

'Thanks.'

'Don't mention it.'

'What's it like being dead?' asked Plughole as the three plodded over the sparse grass in the direction of the track.

116

'You want to know, do you?'

'Yes.'

'Okay,' said Jane. 'We'll tell you.'

Chapter 22

'Actually, Plug,' grinned Delia, 'I'm sorry to disappoint you, but we're still alive.'

'But you're luminous!'

'Glow-in-the-dark spray, Plug, our own invention!'

'Well,' Jane chimed in, 'the spray part's our invention. I sent off for some glow-in-the-dark cream, you see, Plug, because I've always wanted to glow in the dark.'

'Me too,' agreed Delia, 'I've always felt sort of boring at night, you know, not glowing.'

'But the trouble with cream is – you have to *smear* it on so you can't glow all over very easily,' Jane continued eagerly. 'That's how we came to invent the spray. We got a little squirt for squirting spray at greenflies and things and mixed up the cream with water and put it in the squirt, see?'

'I've been carrying it about all day waiting for night to fall – anyway it turned out rather useful.'

'But how can you be alive if Slow drowned you in your sacks?' Plughole demanded to know.

'If she had drowned us, we wouldn't be

alive, Plughole.'

'No, we'd be drowned dead, Plug.'

'But I saw her heave you in. I heard the splashes.'

'So did we. But we were out of those sacks ages before she chucked them down the mine,' explained Jane intently.

'Yes,' agreed Delia. 'The sacks she chucked were full of rubbish, Plug, from litter bins, with the odd rock to make them heavy. You see they let me out of my sack and took me to the phone box to speak to Mum...'

'To rattle her...'

'Yes, to put the frighteners on her. Mark you, I was pretty frightened myself. Anyway after the phone call they took me back to the camp at the mineshaft and bunged me back into my sack...'

'Only they never tied her hands up properly...'

'They didn't tie them up at all – so I was free to yank at the top string, you see, from inside. And as soon as Slow went for a wee...'

'Behind a gorse bush...'

'I broke free...'

'And rescued me...'

'There were these litter bin sacks...'

'Full of litter...'

'So we shoved them into our sacks to make it seem we were still there...'

'And we beetled off...'

'Or, rather, we were in the process of beetling when the rest of them returned with you, dear Plug. So we stayed and watched.'

'Yes. And we realised, Plug, that you were in a jam; so I said, "Now is the time for the glow-in-the-dark lark," I said. It was my idea, you see, Plughole. I'm not just a ...'

'— a ghastly face. But I thought of it too, actually. Anyway it worked, we scared them off and saved you. Good grief! Look, a fire engine!'

A fire engine was indeed careering down the track towards them.

'Stop!' yelled Delia waving her arms.

Plughole saw a familiar face in a nightcap peering out of the cab behind the driver's head.

This large, red face closely resembled a hunk of badly carved ham and belonged to Police Constable Bumsore. The firemen had insisted that he came with them. The dismounted policeman gazed through the glimmering dawn light at the three children. Then an expression of surprise slid over his hamsome face. If you can imagine a hunk of ham looking amazed — then that is what he looked like.

Bumsore's mouth opened and his voice came out of it in an angry, accusing, startled tone. 'It's him,' he yelled, 'the great, big baby burglar!'

Chapter 23

It was bright and tidy at the Littlebampton Police Station; Lightning had been shampooed, the back room had been spring cleaned; yes, everything had been scrubbed and polished — apart from Constable Sloth, and now the two prisoners were about to start on him as he snored gently in his comfortable corner.

'Careful you don't wake 'im up,' ordered the gleaming sergeant. 'We don't wake him until it's time for him to go to bed.'

'Do we have to go to prison? Can't we stay here at the police station keeping it clean?' asked one of the prisoners slowly.

''Course you can't,' replied the sergeant, ''Course you've got to go to prison. Prison is where you belong.'

'What about me?' asked the other prisoner.

'You, being a boy, will be sent to a specially strict school for evil boys.'

'But you said I was a *baby* burglar, not a boy burglar.'

'You were a boy burglar disguised as a baby and you were working for a most dangerous gang of crooks...'

'But they tricked me! It's not fair!'

'No,' agreed Slow. 'They tricked me too and I have got to go to prison. Prison is worse than some soft school for evil boys. I do not like prison; there is lumps in the custard and the smell is not very nice. It smells like the monkey house at the zoo.'

'My mum and dad are...are...' Plughole had been going to say that his mum and dad were in prison but thought better of it.

'What are your mum and dad?' asked Slow. 'I thought you didn't have a mum and dad. I thought you was an orphan.'

'I do have a mum and dad,' replied Plughole firmly. 'They are clowns.'

'Batty took me to a circus to see clowns on my birthday when I was fifty,' smiled Slow. 'I had an *I am 50* badge. When Batty saw the clowns she had an artful plan and she sneaked round and nicked a pair of clown suits from a caravan...'

'What!' cried Plug. He stopped shining Sloth's shoes and gaped up at Slow's empty loo face.

'Yeh,' replied the dim one, 'and next morning Batty and Granny dressed up as clowns and robbed a bank with the blunderbuss. Sludge was the getaway driver and I was look-out. I looked out, see, out the window.'

'You mean they dressed up in real

clowns' costumes?'

'Yeh. Then Batty put them back.'

'Back in the caravan?'

'Yes. And the noses – she put them back too. She is artful, Batty is. Batty and Granny are ever so cunning – and they think I am thick.'

'But you *are* thick,' explained the sergeant.

'Yeh. I have always been thick.'

'You mean Batty put the clown suits back in the caravan so that it would look as if the real clowns had robbed the bank?' Plughole demanded to know.

'Yeh!'

'But my mum and dad were arrested for robbing a bank. They've been in jail for years.'

'Tough.'

'It's not fair!'

'It's not fair me going to prison when Sludge has got all the money. I hope Granny and Batty find her.'

'What will happen if they do?' asked the luckless lad.

'Revenge,' replied the slow one simply.

As you know, Sludge had driven off in Amelia Blight's Rolls Royce in order to become beautiful. You will be glad to hear that she had found her way to the poshest face doctor in London and, while Plughole and Slow were dusting the Littlebampton Police Station, he was looking into her hideous face, working out an estimate, and listening to what she had to say.

'I want to be pretty,' she told him, 'and willowy. I want my face lifted and my bottom shrunk; I want a sweet, dainty little nose and my ears trimmed and pinned back.' She looked intently at the beauty doctor to see if he was paying attention. He was a grey man in a grey suit; he stroked his grey beard and gazed at Sludge through gold-rimmed spectacles. Every now and then he picked up a golden pen and made a short note in quick, neat handwriting.

Massive bum — might need a bacon slicer — that was one of the notes.

The face doctor looked sharply into Sludge's tiger eyes. 'Are you sure you can pay for all this?' he asked bluntly. 'I am an extremely expensive surgeon — £500 an hour and double on Saturdays.'

'How much will it all cost?' grinned the Sludge hoisting a large case onto her knees.

'One hundred thousand pounds,' was the crisp answer.

'Peanuts,' replied the smirking dinner lady. She opened the case and began counting out

£50 notes. He picked up one of them and examined it suspiciously. 'What sort of mug do you take me for?' he snapped. 'This isn't real money!'

'What do you mean?'

'Look at it.'

'Looks real to me.' Sludge picked up a note and scrutinised it closely. 'The Queen is winking,' she admitted. 'That's all that's wrong with it.'

'No it's not. It says BANK OF FUN instead of Bank of England. This is joke money!'

'Joke!' roared the dinner lady rearing up like an angry elephant. 'Well, I'm not laughing!' She picked up her case and swept out of the consulting rooms, down the steps into the street.

The grey man sat shaking his grey head as he watched through the window while the huge hag clambered into her Rolls Royce and sped away. Now what? Sludge asked herself as she honked the horn and foot-slammed forward. Something cold and hard was suddenly pressed into her neck.

'Keep driving,' croaked a familiar voice.

'We want a little chat,' cackled another.

'You was wanting to fix your face, weren't you?' chuckled Granny; she and Batty had

127

sneaked into the back of the Rolls while Sludge had been consulting the face doctor.

'Yeh,' agreed Sludge. 'I suppose you guessed where I'd go first.'

'Well,' sniggered Batty, 'we'll fix your face.'

'Yeh, you won't recognise yourself,' croaked Granny.

'But it'll be expensive,' warned Batty.

'Yes. It'll cost exactly one million quid,' grinned Granny. 'Now, Sludge, about your face...'

Chapter 24

'Honestly, Delia, I feel so helpless – the house is being auctioned...'

'And all the forests and farms...'

'Yes, this time tomorrow we won't have a forest or a farm left.'

'Or even a tree.'

'Or a leaf!'

'And poor Plughole is going to be carted off to some miserable prison for evil boys...'

'And he's not particularly evil!'

'He's not evil at all! In a world full of evil boys, Plughole stands out as completely innocent.'

'It's unjust!'

'It is.'

'We should do something about it while he's still at Littlebampton cop shop...'

'Something daring...'

'...and brilliant.'

'Yes.'

'But what?'

The sadly sighing, fiendish but deeply flummoxed Blighters were lolling gracefully in the Music Room at Blight Hall nibbling crusts and sipping mugs of tap water.

'We could bribe the cops to let him out; that's what people usually do in these circumstances.'

'But we haven't any money.'

'Actually, Jane, we've got stacks of it; remember all that joke money we sent off for?'

'That wouldn't fool them; the Queen's winking.'

'Yes, and it says *Bank of Fun* in huge letters; you're right, even the Littlebampton police would smell a rat.'

'They'd arrest us.'

'Yes, we'd be sent to a cheerless prison for evil girls.'

'Any other ideas?'

'Yes, how about baking a cake with a pistol inside and sending it to Plug so that he could bust his way out?'

'But Plughole isn't the sort of chap that'd be able to bust his way out of prison – even with a gun. He's too good natured.'

'Not evil enough.'

'No.'

'We'll have to bust him out ourselves...'

'With a gun!'

'Precisely.'

'We can help ourselves to Batty's disguise wigs.'

'And her masks...I'll be Princess Diana...'

'And I'll be Fergie.'

'We can use the machine gun water pistol. It's extremely realistic.'

'Okay. When will we do it?'

'Tonight — we'll strike at 0300 hours!'

The pale moon peeped through the bars of Plughole's cell casting a grid of shadows on the wall. The sleepless boy was weary, but worry had woken him for he knew that however grim it was in a cell at Littlebampton Police Station, it would be a million times worse in the prison for evil boys — and he was going to be sent there in the morning.

In fact, it was quite cosy at the police station; Constable Bumsore had supervised Plughole that afternoon and there had been crumpets and mugs of tea when they'd finished mucking out Lightning's stable. In their sleepy way, the Littlebampton police were kind to him — as if they knew he was telling the truth about being tricked and felt sorry for him because of his mum and dad. Thinking about his parents made poor Plughole cry — when would he see them again?

'Pete old chap!' called a familiar voice.

'I must have gone to sleep and be dreaming,' sighed the unfortunate boy. 'And I can smell the smell of Lightning's muck-out muck wafting through the bars of my cell – I'm dreaming in smellovision!'

'Peter darling!' cried his mum.

A key turned. Bolts were drawn. The heavy cell door creaked open.

'There he is,' said the sergeant in his deeply sympathetic voice – the one he used for widows and little girls that were lost. 'I expect he thinks he's dreaming.'

'He's not the only one,' replied Plughole's dad as he watched the startled boy being hugged by his mother.

'You've got me to thank for this,' explained the sergeant modestly as they sat in the ops room later. Plughole was in Bumsore's easy chair and the two famous clowns had their arms around him. 'I persuaded Slow to sign a statement – well make a mark to a statement – saying you was tricked into being a burglar and how it was the Dinner Lady Gang that did the bank raid your mum and dad was done for. I didn't tell you because I didn't want to raise your hopes – but because of Slow's statement you are free to go...'

'And the Queen ordered our release from prison,' explained the clown (his mouth was most Muppet-like as you'd expect from Plughole's dad).

'We will get compensation for being wrongly

imprisoned,' said his mum – whose mouth was good for kissing Plughole better.

'We could start up a little circus of our own,' suggested the dad with his deep clown voice. 'What do you say, Pete, a little circus with three clowns – one of them quite small – or would you rather be sent to school to be a scholar?'

'Don't tease him,' smiled the happy mum – she was opening her mouth to say something motherly when a tremendous BANG shook the police station. It was as if someone had blown open the front door with a blunderbuss. Then three wild figures hurled themselves into the ops room.

'There's the boy,' croaked the one with the gun. 'Grab 'im!'

Chapter 25

'Whatdya curtsey for?' bellowed Sludge accusingly; her face was a perilous purple. The four dinner ladies were together once again in Slow's dark cell, which was in the basement of Littlebampton Police Station. It was crowded in there and Sludge had stepped into Slow's potty which had not improved her temper – or the atmosphere.

''Course I flaming well curtseyed,' replied Granny fiercely. 'I'm surprised you didn't too, my girl. When the Princess of Wales bounds up to you – you gotta curtsey!'

'Not if she's waving a gun.'

'I was taken aback,' croaked the leader defensively. 'Anyway, I've always liked the Royal Family – ever since we nicked the Crown Jewels.'

'You should've shot her!'

'I was going to – only I felt it would not be right to shoot a princess without curtseying first.'

'But when you went and curtseyed the blunderbuss pointed at the floor,' snarled Sludge.

'Only for a second...'

'And that big bloke with the mouth put his flaming great foot on it and kicked it out your hand.'

'Yeh,' agreed Granny. 'Then he kicked me and the Princess stuck 'er gun into me gut and the Fergie one gives Plughole a kiss...'

'She weren't a real Fergie,' yelled Sludge.

'We know,' said Batty soothingly. 'We know they wasn't real, but it all happened so sudden—we thought they were real when they came bursting in. It takes a second or two, Sludge, for people to cotton on...'

'And you're supposed to be the clever ones!'

'At least we don't double-cross our mates,' hissed Batty.

'I may have tried to double-cross you,' replied the Sludge, 'but this evens the score—Granny's dropped us in it.'

'We came close though,' mused Batty wistfully.

'Close to what?' asked Slow. 'Do you mean Sludge came close to my potty?'

'I mean we came close to bringing it all off,' replied the artful one, 'to finding the million quid; Plug was talking...'

''E was singing like an Italian canary,' agreed Granny. 'He told us where 'e 'ad it 'id soon as we put the frighteners on 'em.'

'Fancy him hiding it in his trunk-bed,'

grumbled Sludge.

'Such an obvious place,' agreed Batty. 'And now they've gone off to the big house to get it and give it all back to that 'orrible old bag who don't deserve it.'

'She don't deserve nothing,' muttered Granny.

'And we looked after her so well. Dedicated we was...the way you kept washing your feet, Granny, and the recipes you made up—drunken beef that was a good one.'

'Yes,' agreed Granny, 'a bull's bum boiled in beer.'

'She was surprised by it,' laughed Batty.

'Not as surprised as the bull,' grinned Granny.

'They can't all be gone off to the big house,' said Slow suddenly. 'Listen! I can hear a horrid noise—someone is having a bath upstairs.'

'That's not a bath,' cried Batty. 'That's Plughole laughing!'

Batty was absolutely right; the whirling, swirling sounds of hoots and honks echoed about the ops room. There had not been enough room in the police car for everyone, so the three clowns had remained behind; one had a desperate bath laugh, another a little sweet tin basin laugh, and the third sounded

137

as if treacle was trickling down a drain.

'The way that Granny and Co. swept in,' hooted Plughole.

'Full of threats,' chuckled his mum.

'About what they'd do unless Peter told them where he'd hidden the cash,' honked his dad.

'But what did you mean when you said it was in your trunk-bed,' asked his mum, then she frowned as Plughole explained about sleeping in a trunk instead of a bed.

'I hid the money there when Aunt Amelia said she thought they might not be satisfied with the million pounds but ask for more,' explained the little lad. 'The twins had all this joke money in their joke store; it's very realistic – except the Queen's winking – but I didn't think they'd notice that in the dark.'

'Wasn't it great,' honked the clown, 'when the Princess of Wales burst in waving a tommy gun!'

'That one was Delia,' explained Plughole who was one of the very few people on planet Earth who could tell the Blighters apart.

'It was Delia in the Princess Diana mask.'

'They're both very pretty,' observed his mum – the twins had taken the masks off, of course, when the dinner ladies were safely locked up. They had introduced themselves politely to their uncle and aunt.

'My God,' they'd squawked at the dad, 'you look even more like a Muppet than Plughole!'

'Well, Peter old chap,' said the dad, 'have you decided about what you want to do – go away to school or help us run a circus?'

Once again the three clowns shook with mirth while loud and long and madly strong, Plughole's bath-laugh led the rest.

David Tinkler

THE HEADMASTER WENT SPLAT!

'Kevin Twerp,' hissed Killer Keast, the ferocious headmaster of Shambles School, 'I want to see you in my room immediately.'

Suddenly, it seemed to go cold. The light went dim. There was a gasp from the children and the teachers shivered. Kevin felt faint and his mouth went dry.

Kevin Twerp's life hasn't been easy; pop-singing dad killed in an air crash, Mum – Nitty Norah the Hair Explorer – driven out to work as a school nurse. And, looming, like a dark shadow, Killer Keast.

But, with the help of WPC Rose Button, lodger and All-England Mud Wallowing Champion, things *will* change . . .!

Another Knight Book

David Tinkler

THE CASE OF THE FEEBLE WEEBLE

Think about your own dear school. Is it shabby and in need of a lick of paint? Are the teachers a bane and a pain?

Well, Shambles School is EVEN WORSE! However mad and bad your head teacher may be, he or she is meek and mild compared with Killer Keast.

From the author of THE HEADMASTER WENT SPLAT! and THE SCOURGE OF THE DINNER LADIES, another outrageous school detective story featuring the extraordinary Twerp family, Policewoman Rose Button and, of course, Killer Keast, the most feared Headmaster in the universe.

Another Knight Book

David Tinkler

THE SCOURGE OF THE DINNER LADIES

CHOMP CHOMP BURP SLURP

This was the noise of dinner time.
Nobody dared to talk.

'Who was that?' yelled Mrs Sludge.

'WHO WAS WHISPERING?'

There were some tough new dinner ladies
at Littlesprat Primary School: The
Granny Fang Gang. Mrs Sludge was the
roughest, toughest dinner lady that there
has ever been. And now she was
brandishing her ladle!

Could the pupils of Littlesprat survive
The Scourge of the Dinner Ladies?

Another Knight Book

David Tinkler

THE DINNER LADIES CLEAN UP

The Dinner Ladies are back – the fiercest, wickedest, ugliest crime gang in the country. They have kidnapped Caroline Crisp, stolen the trophies of the Metropolitan Dance Display Team, and now they are after the greatest prize of all – the Queen's Crown Jewels.

Can Caroline stop them, with only the help of Miss Thrasher's inflatable pantaloons?

MORE GREAT BOOKS AVAILABLE
FROM KNIGHT